# Femdom Sexy Surprises

**Sexy Surprises, Volume 50**

Giselle Renarde

Published by Giselle Renarde, 2024.

# Table of Contents

# Femdom Sexy Surprises

*6 Erotic Stories*

Giselle Renarde

# Too Old For This

Did Larissa still believe what she'd said all those years ago? Maybe she'd changed her mind since then. Hopefully she had…

"Let me see that pretty pussy."

Minnie's eyes nearly jumped out of their sockets. "Shhh! People will hear you."

Larissa cocked her head. "So shut the door."

There was so much work piled up on her desk—cheques to cut and invoices to follow up on—but Minnie couldn't say no. When Larissa got that gleam in her eye, all those pressing office concerns snapped away like the crack of a whip. Anyway, it was Larissa's company. If the boss wanted the door closed, Minnie would just have to close the door.

"Turn down the blinds," Larissa said, her sharp canines gleaming. "Then park your ass on my desk. You know the drill."

"Yes, Boss." Minnie fumbled with the blinds. If she took too long, she might incur an unbearable punishment. "Sorry, Boss. The thing is sticky."

"*The thing*? Is it really?" Larissa pushed her chair back, closer to the window. No blinds on that one, and it ran carpet to ceiling. Even on the twenty-eighth floor, Minnie wondered if other office workers in other office towers diddled themselves as they watched her daily submission. Seemed unlikely, but maybe someone out there had a telescope?

Anyway, if anyone really was watching, their eyes would no doubt be glued to Larissa. Minnie felt like she'd aged twenty years in the past five, but her boss only grew more striking with age. At thirty-six, Minnie's auburn curls were dappled with greys while Larissa's straightened hair ran jet-black along her scalp, pulled tightly into a golden clip, long extensions cascading down her back. No wrinkles marring the dark skin under those blazing eyes.

Larissa could have been a supermodel. Hell, she still could be. If there were beauty pageants for business executives, she could strut across the stage in that sharp suit jacket and fearsome leather skirt. Crisp white shirt, jewels and gold. She'd take top prize.

Minnie swished around the office in her summer skirt before hopping on Larissa's desk. Ooh, was she ever wet! When did that happen? Seemed like every time Larissa gave her that hungry look, her pussy swelled, her clit throbbed, and hot juice spilled down her thighs.

"Open your legs, little miss."

Her throat ran dry, but she hiked her feet off the carpet and hooked her heels into the drawer handles. The veneer on Larissa's mid-century modern desk was scuffed in two spots, from Minnie's two feet: small black stripes from every pair of heels she'd ever worn.

"Wider." Larissa pointed back and forth between both knees. "Wide as you can."

"Yes, Boss." Minnie parted her thighs until her muscles screamed. "How's that?"

"It'll have to do," Larissa faux-clucked. "Now hike up your skirt."

Minnie took the diaphanous fabric between her fingers and thumbs, tossing it around to tease her boss. "Up?"

"All the way." A bit of a growl, now. "Up past your hips. Then unbutton your blouse and lean back."

Hiking up her wispy skirt, Minnie imagined what her boss must be seeing. She could tell by the hot gleam in Larissa's eyes when she'd lifted far enough. Larissa was the type to play her cards close to the chest, but Minnie could always tell when the wolf caught sight of its sweet prey.

"Good," Larissa said, almost a sneer. "No panties. Very nice."

"And the garters, Boss? Do you like the stockings and garters?"

Larissa's expression hardened. "Don't push your luck."

Ooh, Minnie had really gotten to her today! The garters were always a hit.

"Unbutton that blouse." Leaning forward, Larissa grabbed a letter opener from her desk. The weapon had a thick jade handle. Minnie had met it before. "Quick, or I'll slice those buttons off and you'll have to walk around all day with your top hanging open."

"You love making me blush, don't you, Boss?"

Minnie was really pushing her luck. She knew that. But if she got off on praise, she got off even more on admonitions.

"You'd like that," Larissa sneered. "Having to walk these halls with your bra showing, your tits hanging out. You like it when people stare. You want to be the center of attention."

"No, Boss. Not at all."

"Think you can fool me?" Tracing the letter opener around Minnie's top button, Larissa somehow managed to drive it into the hole and pop it off. The button went flying across the room, landing on Larissa's abandoned office chair.

"Oh no."

Larissa's expression darkened. "You love it."

"I'll do the rest." Minnie's fingers trembled as she slipped the next button through its hole. Not easy to undress on demand, even after all these years. She wanted to please Larissa, impress her. Strippers make it look so easy.

Her bra was white lace, and it captured Larissa's gaze even though she'd worn it many times before.

"You like?" Minnie asked, propping her breasts up with both hands. "If you look, you can just make out a hint of my nipples through the pattern. Can you see them?"

"Peachy," Larissa said, nodding. She traced the hazardous end of her letter opener down the curve of Minnie's breast, right near the border of lace.

"Cold." Minnie tried not to shiver. Goosebumps rose across her bare flesh as her boss' weapon teased her skin. "Feels good."

"Oh?" Larissa turned the letter opener forty-five degrees, digging the dull edge into her breast. "Is that better?"

The metal wasn't sharp. It jabbed Minnie in a way that made her crave more intense pain. She thrust her tits forward, driving them against the edge, watching her skin indent around the dull blade. Her boss refused to cut her with anything sharp. She'd asked before.

Larissa traced the warming metal against the lace edge of her bra, drawing it away from her skin, but only slightly. "Pull down the cups. I want to see your tits."

She said it like she'd never seen them before... like she hadn't touched them, licked them, felt them, bitten them, every workday for the past five years. Like Minnie's body was new and exciting. Every day, when she exposed her breasts to her employer, it was new and exciting all over again. This never got old.

Larissa didn't often remove clothing, so Minnie's breath caught when she unbuttoned her tailored suit jacket. Without taking it off, she slipped open her top, like its buttons were magnets she only had to slide her fingers across to undo.

Her tits were small. She didn't wear a bra, didn't need one, especially when her jackets always covered up her chest. Her brown skin shone in the afternoon sun, which reflected off the business sector's many mirrored windows.

Minnie watched in unsanctioned awe as her boss' dark nipples puckered, hardened to sharp buds. She didn't know what to say when Larissa drew closer, pressing those pointed nipples to hers. Their tits touched, and a bolt of arousal travelled Minnie's body, swirling like a maelstrom in her belly. Larissa's erect nipples pressed into her softer skin, teasing her, taunting her, making her feverish.

"What are you craving?" Larissa asked.

Her pussy ached. She couldn't speak.

"Nothing?" Larissa's mouth was so close Minnie could feel her boss' breath in her ear. "You mean your pussy isn't wet for me? Your nipples don't want to be sucked?"

Minnie's throat ran dry. She tried to tell her boss how badly she wanted her pussy fucked, but no sound came out. Hot juice dripped from her cunt, down her ass crack, soaking her skirt. She'd have a wet spot there, just like every other day. There was a reason she bought skirts with busy floral patterns—so her co-workers wouldn't notice the splotches of nectar soaking through.

"What about this?" Larissa asked, holding the letter opener by its blade. "You want me to fuck you with it?"

Nodding, Minnie pushed a faint sound past her lips: "Please."

Why did she get so nervous? Every day? She should be used to this by now. It shouldn't be so enthralling, but every morning she dressed for a hot date and came into work with her heart battering her ribs. Though she was in and out all day, each time she set foot in her boss' office, her clit throbbed. Would this be the time Larissa made a pass at her? Asked her to close the door?

Minnie never took initiative. She always waited to be told what to do. At this point, it was like Larissa had a responsibility to her. Her employer paid biweekly, provided free coffee, and took care of her sexual needs. A sweet deal, but Minnie couldn't help worrying their arrangement would come to a screeching halt at any moment.

Dragging her hard nipples down Minnie's bare belly, Larissa said, "I can follow the smell of your cunt. It's especially strong today."

"Is it?" Minnie felt her cheeks light up. "I don't know why."

"Did you wash for me this morning?"

"Of course. I always do."

"Were you running around a lot?"

Minnie hesitated. Back and forth between the bank and the post office? Yes, she'd been on her feet all day.

"I can smell your sweat." Larissa snatched a wet wipe from her desk drawer and cleaned the thick jade handle of her letter opener. "Hot pussy and perspiration, you bad girl. You dirty girl. Are you trying to put me off?"

"No, Boss. I'm sorry."

Grabbing another wipe, Larissa rubbed it over Minnie's wet pussy. "I shouldn't have to do this—clean you like a baby. It's your responsibility to stay sweet for me."

"I know." Minnie's heartbeat thundered in her ears as Larissa tossed the wipes in the trash. "Tomorrow I'll smell sweet as pie."

"Good." Larissa circled the rounded jade around Minnie's slit, not quite pressing it in, not quite touching her clit. "How does that feel, hmm?"

Minnie swallowed hard. "Tickles."

"Tickles?"

"Teases." Her breath came on so fast her exposed breasts surged against her pulled-down bra. "It's not enough. I want more."

"More?" A wicked smirk crossed Larissa's painted lips.

"I want it inside me."

"Inside?"

"In my pussy." Leaning back on her elbows, Minnie cradled her breasts with both hands. "I want you to shove it up my snatch and fuck me with it."

"Push your tits together." Larissa's dark brown nipples seemed to harden as she spoke. "Roll them between your fingers. That's right." She nudged Minnie's clit with the jade handle, just gently, not exerting nearly enough pressure. But she knew what she was doing. "Now raise those big breasts to your lips. Suck them."

Minnie's clit throbbed against the mint-green rock. She wrapped her mouth around one swollen nipple, and felt her tongue's velvet heat soaring from her breast all the way down to her sopping wet pussy.

"Your *breasts*." Larissa whacked Minnie's pussy lips, using the letter opener like a club. "Both of them. Both at once."

"Both?" Minnie's brain buzzed as jade spankings struck her mound. "Both my tits? In my mouth?"

"Yes," Larissa said. "Suck them both."

Holding her heavy breasts against her chin, Minnie bowed her head and opened her mouth. She squeezed her tits together until they met against her tongue, and then closed her lips around both nipples. She'd never done this before. It felt strange for a moment, trying to suckle two tits at once, but the second she found her groove, liquid pleasure travelled her veins, filling her body with swirling gushes of heat. Her skin tingled and her muscles trembled. She gazed beseechingly at her boss as she sucked both breasts.

Larissa slipped the letter opener between her slick pussy lips and entered her with the bulging knob of jade. Minnie's cunt had no memory, when it came to fucking. Every time felt like the first. Her slit was tight and reluctant, but her juice coated the makeshift cock as it forged a path between her thighs.

"How does it look?" Minnie wanted to ask, but she worried Larissa would be displeased if she stopped sucking her tits. She wished she had a better view as her boss filled her pussy with jade.

"I don't like this. Get down," Larissa instructed. "Both feet on the floor. Both tits on the desk."

Minnie whimpered because it felt so good, sucking both nipples. She didn't want to stop. But if that's what Larissa wanted...

"Like this?" she asked once she'd climbed down and inverted herself.

"Hands behind your back." Larissa tucked Minnie's summer skirt under her arms, and then yanked the waist of her garter belt over her wrists. "Can you escape?"

"I could if I wanted to," Minnie admitted. "But I don't want to."

Minnie could see her boss' expression in her mind's eye: impressed and satisfied. Then Larissa grabbed Minnie's hair and yanked it until her breasts rose off the desk. "What about now?"

"I still don't want to escape," Minnie said. "Really, I just want you to fuck me."

A long moment passed, and all Minnie could feel was her hair pulling sharply on her scalp. The blinding pain made her cringe, and her pussy tightened as the letter opener found it. Larissa chuckled as she forced the bulge of jade deeper into Minnie's cunt, like this was funny.

"Again," Minnie begged when her boss bottomed out. "Slow. And twist it."

Her breast sat like heavy cushions against the desk, supporting her while she leaned back. The garter elastic cut into her wrists, but nothing hurt as much as she wanted it to. Not even the steady thumping of jade as it rammed her tight cunt.

Every so often, Larissa stopped fucking her, pausing with the handle inside her snatch. Her boss swirled the jade cock, moving it in roving circles, making it feel larger, like the hard rock was expanding her slit. The blade must be digging into Larissa's palm by now. Minnie only wished it was digging into hers. Even without a cutting edge, that slicing pain would feel wonderful.

"I'm about to make you come," Larissa said.

With nothing but a letter opener? Minnie seriously doubted that, but she said nothing, just listened as her boss opened a desk drawer and fished around for something. She didn't get a chance to see it before she heard a buzz and Larissa pressed something smooth and relatively flat over her mound.

"Oh my God!" Minnie cried.

Larissa let go of the letter opener just long enough to smack her ass. "Quiet down. You want your co-workers to know what you're up to in here?"

"No, no, no..."

The vibrating thing, whatever it was, pulled an orgasm out of her, easy as sucking a milkshake through a straw. She bit her lip and clamped down on the jade cock, but that only intensified her climax. She whimpered, struggling not to, but unable to keep the little whinnies inside.

"You want the whole office talking about you?" Larissa scolded. "They'll say you slept your way to success. They'll whisper *dyke* when you walk by. They'll joke about you licking the boss-lady's girly parts. Is that what you want, Minnie?"

Vibrations travelled her arms and legs like little bolts of lightning, finding her fingers and toes, making them dance with arousal. Larissa fucked her so hard it hurt and finally, finally, Minnie got a taste of the pain she craved.

"Oh God!" Minnie squealed. "Hurts. Feels so good."

Larissa slapped her ass. "Keep your voice down."

"No!" She'd never rebelled like this before, but her pleasure and pain mingled with fear of rejection. "I don't care who knows. You do! You care!"

She cringed, expecting Larissa to smack her ass silly, but not a single blow landed. She waited, but nothing. Her belly whirled and buzzed. Her thighs trembled. The vibrator between her thighs brought on wave after wave of orgasm, and she folded her face against her breasts to muffle the sound.

Larissa turned the jade knob like a corkscrew, withdrawing it slowly from the Minnie's swollen cunt. She panted viciously, rising and falling as her breasts pressed firmly into the desk. Her boss was strangely silent, almost absent.

Tearing her tingling hands from the waist of her garter, she turned sharply to meet Larissa's vacant stare. "Did I do something? What's wrong?"

"What did you mean when you said that I care?" Larissa asked. "You think I'm ashamed of something?"

Minnie wasn't sure how to answer. Leaning back against the desk, she caught a glimpse of the vibrator in her boss' hand and wanted to ask about it—the toy was green and looked like a leaf—but now was not the time.

"You think I'm ashamed of *us*?"

Without meaning to, Minnie nodded. "Only because... well, don't you remember? When we first started this, you kept telling me it wasn't serious, we weren't a couple. You said we were getting too old for this, and if we were still at it when you turned fifty you'd kill yourself."

Larissa's jaw dropped. She said nothing.

"You don't remember?"

She shook her head. "I was young. I was stupid."

"So when you had your birthday the other week, I thought..." Tears bit Minnie's hot throat. She tried not to cry. "I've just been waiting..."

"I'm so sorry." Larissa wrapped her long arms around Minnie, bringing their bare breasts together. "What a *stupid* thing to say."

"Then it isn't true?"

"Of course not." Her boss petted her hair, breathing warmly in her ear. "It wasn't easy for me, coming to terms with being kinky, being queer. I fought it for a long time, even after we started this. People look at me, even other lesbians, and they say, 'You must be straight. You're just messing around. You're just experimenting.' Nobody was there for me. Nobody but you."

Minnie hugged her hard, squeezing their bodies together until tears burst out.

As Larissa offered sweet words of consolation, Minnie sobbed on her shoulder—tears of joy, tears of relief.

She would never be too old to cry.

# Bondage on a First Date

Did Pella realize the balls it took to ask her out?

It wasn't easy. Didn't matter that they flirted at work every day. Eric felt like he was going to throw up when he invited Pella to dinner and a movie.

Thank God she'd said yes. If she'd turned him down, he would have quit his job, or stabbed himself with a letter opener. It wouldn't just have been humiliating. Eric would have felt... well, heartbroken.

Guys weren't supposed to care or whatever but, hell, he wasn't made of stone.

Standing on the wrong side of Pella's door, Eric cupped his hand over his nose and checked his breath. Minty fresh. Perfect. Still, his stomach flipped when he reached up to knock.

*Be strong.*

He made a fist and rapped at the door.

*You never get a second chance to make a first impression.*

Eric's heart stopped as he waited for Pella.

He could hear her on the other side, shuffling, jiggling the handle.

When the door finally opened, she wasn't there.

"Pella? It's Eric. Where are you?"

"Behind the door," she said without emerging. "Come in for a sec."

"Oh. Okay, thanks."

Eric stepped over the threshold, and the first thing he noticed was a warm scent, like cinnamon and pears. Pella's apartment was really dark inside. Even when she'd closed the door behind him, Eric strained to find her shape in the shadows.

"Take off your shoes," she said. "I just got new area rugs."

"Oh yeah, you were saying." Eric scuttled out of his shoes without untying the laces. "From the Persian shop on Yorkville, right? Those places scare the crap out of me."

"Persian places?"

"No, no, I meant boutiques." His heart raced. Pella must know by now that he didn't have anything against her culture or ethnicity, whatever you call it. "Fancy stores freak me out. I always feel like they're gonna give me the bum's rush because they don't like my pants."

"Your pants?"

Pella took a step forward, and Eric took a step back. As she forced him into the candlelit living room, he got his first look at what she had on: black silk, with ribbons criss-crossing her front. Very short. *Very* short. That wasn't a dress, was it? It wasn't something you'd wear out of the house.

Eric swallowed hard. "Oh, you're not... ready?"

"I'm ready," she said, almost a growl.

He knew he was staring at her cleavage, but he couldn't help himself. Pella never dressed like this for work—low-cut, silky, seductive. Her legs were completely bare, from her thighs down to... actually, she did have shoes on: open-toed, with little heels and black straps. Her toenails were painted with dark polish. Purple, maybe? Hard to tell in the candlelight.

"You're ready... to...go out?"

Pella threw her head back and laughed. Rather than answer, she pressed him across the room, unzipping his pants and letting them fall down his legs. What was she doing? Taking off his underwear?

Was this really happening, or had he hit his head on the way over?

In the darkness, Eric had no idea where he was stepping. He wasn't entirely surprised when he fell on a couch. Really, the fact that he was naked from the waist down was more of a shock.

"We're here!" Pella cooed. "Happy first date."

"I thought we were going out," he said. "Dinner and a movie."

"Everybody does dinner and a movie." Pella fell to her knees and grabbed hold of a silky black cord. "I thought we might start our evening off with a little light bondage."

Eric's cock surged as he realized what was going on.

She'd planned this, obviously. Pella always was the most organized person in the office, but Eric had never known anyone to be so prepared in the bedroom. Not that they were in her bedroom. No, Pella obviously wanted him on the couch—she'd tied ropes to the heavy wooden feet, and was now in the process of securing those ropes to his ankles.

He let her, of course. He was too shocked to move.

"Put your arms out," Pella instructed. She didn't wait for him to move before grabbing his wrists and stretching them out across the back of the sofa. "Very good. You've done this before."

"I'm pretty sure I haven't," Eric said, chuckling with nerves.

Pella had obviously tied two cords to the back legs of the couch, because now she was tying his wrists up, too.

She knotted the rope tightly. "You've never been bound like this?"

"Not to a couch. Not on a first date." Not at all, but he didn't want to seem like a bondage virgin when Pella was obviously so keen on it.

"How does that feel?" she asked. "Too loose? Too tight?"

"Definitely not too loose." The ropes splayed him like a butterfly, so wide his inner thighs burned. He was open to her, open for her, and it hit him how vulnerable he was. "What were you planning, exactly?"

Pella cocked her head and smiled. "Nervous?"

His cock jumped, drawing her gaze. "Should I be?"

Shuffling between his open thighs, she shrugged. "That depends, I suppose."

"Depends on what?"

She leaned her naked knees against the front of the couch and unbuttoned Eric's stiff shirt, slowly, top to bottom. The pace was torture. What was she planning? He had a few ideas of what might be in store, but Pella worked in mysterious ways.

"Ahh, look at your chest!" She wove her fingers together beneath her chin, smiling rapturously. "My God, you're fit. I thought you'd look good, but this... this is a nice surprise."

Eric's cock waved with delight, and Pella chuckled sweetly. He wanted to return the compliment, but what could he say? *You look good*? You look *great*? Everything sounded stupid, in his mind. With all his blood flowing straight to his crotch, he couldn't form a proper sentence.

"You look... wow..."

Well, it was better than nothing.

"Wow, do I?" Pella fell between his legs, slowly stroking his thighs. "I look wow..."

"Sorry," he said. "My brain is not... thinking."

She grinned and angled her fingers, so the nails caught his skin. She traced them slowly down his thighs, digging just deep enough to make him writhe against his bindings. "I like it. *Wow.* I take that as a compliment."

"It was definitely intended that way," he told her.

His cock lurched at her hand, but she swept it out of the way, teasingly. It landed like felled lumber, splashing precum down his leg. He didn't want to let her see how good that felt, but how could he possibly hide it? She'd got him colossally aroused, tying him up spread-eagle across the couch, then tracing those vicious fingernails across his flesh.

Now she was kneeling between his legs, waiting.

He admired her control and precision. She had this all planned out in her mind, didn't she? Pella knew just what she wanted.

She traced the backs of her fingernails up his thighs, and beyond—up the ridges of his belly, up his chest. When she wrapped her fingers around his neck, the sparkle in her eyes tied Eric's stomach in knots. What was she doing? She wouldn't strangle him. No, she couldn't. Even bound up, he could certainly escape.

Couldn't he?

Pella giggled as she ran her hands down his chest. "You're cute when you're scared."

"Am I?" Eric didn't want to feel shaken, but this was all new to him. "Thanks."

"What about me?" she asked, planting kisses down the tight, arching muscles of his belly. "Am I cute?"

"Cute, yes. Scared? Doesn't look like it."

Her lip twitched before a smile took over. "Right…"

Eric gazed down at the girl hovering over his hard cock. Pella from the office. Pella, his work friend. His reason for getting up in the morning—not that he'd ever told her that.

As his erection whacked her magnificent cleavage, it occurred to him that she was every bit as apprehensive as he was. She was just better at concealing her fear.

Swallowing hard, Eric raised his hips off the couch, driving his cock into the tight valley between Pella's breasts. He was just riding the surface, but even the slightest touch brought an amazing sensation through his body, from his dick right up to his heart. He'd never felt anything so intense.

"Look at this cock," Pella said in a whisper.

She bowed her head and spit.

As soon as that wet warmth met his red-hot tip, she pressed her thumb against it, rubbing her spit and his precum all over his cockhead. Her hands were everywhere! One clenched tight to the top of his shaft, moving only slightly while the other hand found his balls.

"Oh, for fuck's sake!" Eric threw his head back, but it snapped up again. "What are you doing to me?"

Bending forward, Pella brought her breasts out through the low V-neck of her black silk. Eric's breath hitched as her exposed nipples met the cool evening air. They tightened into dark, pebbled buds. In the candlelight, her flesh glowed like bronze.

Setting her big breasts on Eric's thighs, Pella bowed her head and spit on his dick. Who'd have thought it could feel so good? But, then, who'd have thought a first date would turn into... *this*?

As Pella bent forward, something slipped down her head, falling to the floor, and releasing a waterfall of hair over her perfect shoulders.

"Your scrunchie," Eric said, nodding to the ground. "It fell out. It's right there."

Pella appeared amused. "My scrunchie?" She picked up the black elastic and said, "This? It's not a scrunchie."

"Oh."

"It's a hair band."

"Oh." Eric gazed from her luscious breasts to the elastic in her hand. "What's a scrunchie?"

*Who cares*? Why was he asking stupid questions?

Pella bit her bottom lip, like she was looking up the definition in her mind. "A scrunchie is one of those big hair ties they wore in the '80s. The ones with fabric around them. This is not a scrunchie, it's just an elastic you put around your head to keep hair out of your face."

"Oh." This had to be the longest conversation Eric had ever had about hair products. "Okay."

"It's good for other things too," Pella said, weaving the long elastic around her fingers. She suddenly seemed more interested in the elastic than she was in Eric. He wasn't sure exactly what to do about that.

But his cock wasn't so subtle. It leapt forward to whack Pella's tits, spilling precum across the expanse of her flesh.

"Somebody's eager," she said with a laugh.

"Looks like."

Pella's expression darkened as she took his balls in hand. She gripped them tight, making them strain against his sac. Eric was so shocked he didn't make a sound. He didn't even struggle as she wound her hair elastic around his balls.

At first, it didn't really register what she was up to. She'd already tied up his wrists and his ankles. Now she was tying up his balls?

The strain was like nothing he'd ever felt. It was painful, but it didn't hurt. He felt struck up and weak, but the harder his cock strained, the stronger he felt, too. Nothing made sense.

"How's that?" she asked, though she seemed to know already.

"Good." What else could he say? How was it supposed to feel?

"Ready for more?"

"I don't know..."

She smirked as she wrapped her full breasts around his dick. God, they were warm. Warm and wonderful. His balls strained against the underside of her boobs as she began moving them, just slowly. Slowly gobbling up his entire dick with her full, fleshy breasts. She spit again, and it landed deep inside her cleavage. He could feel it against his throbbing shaft.

"You like that?" she asked.

"How could you tell?"

As her cleavage consumed his cock, Eric tightened his ass cheeks without really meaning to. It was the only way he could thrust.

Every time he squeezed his butt, he felt it through his balls. That bound-up pair clenched tight, driving a strange pleasure through his shaft. He felt huge inside the cavern of Pella's cleavage.

Eric's breath rattled in his lungs. "God, Pella. What are you doing to me?"

She pinched her nipples, and he could have sworn he could feel that too. When she bit her bottom lip, his balls quaked. They were trying to creep up close to his body, he realized, but the band kept them at bay. All he could do was sit there and watch as she fucked him with her tits, riding him hard and hot.

How was she doing that?

And was she enjoying it as much as she seemed to be?

Eric bucked between Pella's beautiful breasts. Hard to believe this was the very first interaction he was having with them. Usually, the sequence went: look, touch, suck, nibble. Fucking might not happen at all, and certainly not on a first date.

"You're killing me," Eric moaned as Pella curled her head down to lick his cockhead. "Oh, for fuck's sake!"

She giggled deep in her throat. Her hair tumbled forward, dancing down the sides of his bare thighs. Jiggling her tits on his erection, she sucked just the tip between her full, luscious lips.

"Christ, I'm gonna come if you keep doing that."

She made a noise that sounded like "Good" without even opening her mouth.

Eric's body didn't feel like his own. It moved of its own volition, bucking against his bindings, throbbing against that not-a-scrunchie.

"Don't you want..." How could he phrase this without sounding full of himself? "I mean, you don't want to...?"

*To fuck me? You don't want to pull up that little silk number and sit on my hot dick?*

Pella moaned around his cockhead, sucking that most sensitive bit while her tits wrapped around him like a tight pussy. Everything about her struck him as elegant—even the way she bounced on his hard-on. It was more like writhing, like an undulating mass of flesh.

God, he loved her curves. What a body! What a great fuck!

Every suck brought him to the brink, but nothing put him over. It must have been the elastic, compressing his balls, keeping his cum from coming out. Without it, he'd have exploded forty times over by now.

"Can you take off the scrunchie?" he asked.

Pella mumbled something around his cock, but he didn't understand.

"I want to come! Please!" Eric clenched his ass and bucked off the couch, getting so close to orgasm he could almost taste it. "You gotta take off the scrunchie!"

Pella jerked up and his cockhead popped out of her mouth. "It's not a scrunchie!"

Her eyes blazed. Eric got the same feeling he'd had when he thought she was going to strangle him. Then a grin broke across her lips, and Eric rolled his eyes. "Fine, then can you take off *the elastic*?"

With a full, toothy smile, Pella said, "Sure."

She didn't even unwrap her breasts from around his cock before digging underneath to fondle his balls.

"Oh, that's good." Eric bucked against her breasts, but they weren't so tight now that her hands were otherwise engaged. "You know what? Leave it."

"Leave it?" Pella wrapped her hands around her huge breasts and hugged his begging cock.

He wasn't sure what she'd done, exactly, but the elastic around his balls felt a little looser. He tested the waters, fucking her tits slowly. Her lips parted gently, and stayed that way, like she was gasping silently. She seemed worlds away, transported by pleasure.

Did this really feel as good for her as it did for him?

Eric planted his feet firmly on the floor. Harnessing all the strength left in his legs, he drove his erection between Pella's breasts so hard his balls lodged themselves somewhere inside her cleavage.

Pella growled like a bear in heat as she plunged her face against her boobs, swallowing as much of Eric's cock as was sticking up between them.

How could she bend that way? How could anyone be so flexible?

She hugged her breasts, squeezing his balls and the root of his cock. How was she doing that? The pressure was immense. She squeezed him tight, like she was trying to squeeze the cum right out of him...

And, fuck, it was working!

Pella mewed and squealed as she sucked his cockhead. Eric's balls pulled up tight to his body—as tight as they could get, considering they were bound up—and Pella pulled away just as he released his first gush.

"Yessss!" she hissed as white cream splattered across her tits. "Oh God, look at all that hot jizz!"

*So dirty!*

Eric shot another load when those smutty words registered. Pella threw her head back and shuddered. Her breasts jiggled around his dick, drawing out more cum. She might as well have been sucking it through a straw!

Letting go of her breasts, Pella dug her fingernails into Eric's thighs and arched back. Yet more cum spilled across her chest, painting white over bronze like a Jackson Pollock canvas.

*Beautiful.*

Pella fell back on her heels, dragging her nails the length of his thighs. His cock strained for her, but he was spent. *Totally* spent. He ached to get hard again, so she could unleash him and wrap her wet pussy around his dick, but that wasn't going to happen. He was gone, exhausted. He could have slept right there, tied to the couch. Easily.

"That was..." Pella shook her head, completely out of breath. "Wow!"

"See? I told you *wow* was a compliment." Eric chuckled, shuffling against the couch. "Do you think you could take off this... scrunchie?"

She smirked, then smacked his thigh. "It's not a scrunchie."

"I know. Just teasing."

When she peeled off the elastic, her touch made him laugh. It tickled. She didn't seem to realize how sensitive his flesh was.

Or maybe she did. Hard to tell...

"We'll probably miss our dinner reservation, but the movie's not until nine." Eric watched keenly as Pella stood between his legs. "Did you still want to go out?"

"I don't know." Pulling off her silk chemise, she stood naked before his bound-up body. "Whatever you like."

# Dressing for Dinner

Wednesday evenings, I dress for dinner.

Shay and I have reached the point where our lives pretty much revolve around the Wednesday routine. I don't think I could get through the first three days of the workweek without the sheer anticipation it generates. Then, of course, I coast through Thursday and Friday on the wings of blissful recollection.

Usually, my wife and I take turns cooking. Not Wednesdays. There's a wonderful service called *Restaurants-To-Go*—the Call Girl of food delivery, Shay says—where you can place a dinner order from any number of fine restaurants in the city and have it brought right to your door. Costs a little more than ordering a pizza, but sometimes you just have to treat yourself.

Dressing for dinner is a ritualistic activity for me. Shay knows I need to do this part alone. From under the bed, I pull out the huge suitcase I keep locked on the off-chance the kids or Shay's dad get nosy when they come to visit. Not that it would seem strange to find a make-up case, some panties, hose, heels, and the like in our bedroom; they could just as easily be Shay's. I guess I'm a little irrational, but it stays locked nonetheless.

Foundation, powder, blush, shadow, mascara, liners—lip and eye—and lipstick all get arranged like toy soldiers in front of the mirror. What have I forgotten? Oh, of course! I still need to shave. Can't do that after I've started with the make-up.

Always a new razor on Wednesdays. A close, attentive shave, and my skin is soft as a baby's bottom.

Every Wednesday is prom night, for me. As I toss my work clothes in the corner, my heart skips. It's incredible how the excitement of dressing never wears off. Sometimes I feel like a child, with this inexorable love of repetition.

Shay loves me in the eggplant-coloured gown, not that she'd ever say so explicitly. I'll wear that tonight. It's a very classy piece. I'd love to be able to wear a thong and not worry about panty lines, but thongs just aren't practical in concealing what I need to conceal. At any rate, my snug-fitting, hip-hugging panties are really quite slimming.

I prefer a pair of classic silk stockings with a stay-up elastic-lace trim. Not particularly practical, but they don't need to be. They look great, feel great, and let my thighs breathe. And the shoes... I must have a nice pair of heels! It's the only time I wear shoes in the house, but the black open-toed heels are a must with this outfit.

Here I'm putting on my heels before I even choose a bra! Breast-forms were another little treat: pricey but worth it, at least for the look. If I'm being honest, they feel more like silicon implants than the real thing, but I love the perky nipples. They show right through my tops.

The doorbell rings and I freeze, clutching my breasts to my chest. It couldn't be Shay's father; he's not due until Saturday. No, of course it isn't. It's the food. Every week I have that same panic moment. You'd think I'd have learned to anticipate it by now.

I laugh until I catch sight of myself in the mirror. It irks me, how ridiculous I look halfway through the process.

Time to start on my face. I won't bore you with the details, as it's quite an intensive undertaking. Time-consuming, too, but I'm hurrying along knowing that dinner's here. Shay will be rightly peeved if she has to eat a cold meal because I can't get my make-up on fast enough.

*My lovely Shay…* I don't know anyone with a wife so special as mine. I'm very lucky to have her. Who else would put up with all this?

Oh, and she's calling me now. Can you hear her? "Get down here, Little Miss! Dinner's on the table."

I'll just finish up my lipstick and toss on the blond wig… perfect! This is one of the rare moments when I actually like what I see in the mirror. Step into this dress and, I must say, I look quite nice. All ready to venture down.

"Well, well, well," Shay sighs as I descend the staircase, one foot in front of the other like a runway model. "Get a load of the little slut in the purple dress."

My heart flutters. I love how I'm always her "little" something. I don't *feel* little.

Shay pulls out my dining chair and slides it in as I take a seat. Her chivalry makes me weak in the knees. Good thing I'm sitting down.

"It's eggplant," I clarify as she sits to my left.

Considering her plate with a confused expression, she says, "It's Pad Thai."

I chuckle. "No, my gown, silly. This isn't purple, it's eggplant."

A hint of a smile crosses her lips, but she buries it in a scowl. "Hurry up and eat. I'm horny as hell, and I'm not paying you to talk."

She's not paying me at all, but I don't say that. All nerves, I pick at my Pad Thai. "I spent good money on your meal," Shay scolds. "Clear your plate or there's no dessert."

Giggling, I push my voice into its most dulcet register. "Yes, Mother."

"Don't get smart with me," she continues as I trap noodles between chopsticks and make every attempt to get them in my mouth. "Messy beast. This is why I can't take you out for dinner. You're an embarrassment."

"But a *pretty* embarrassment," I chime in, patting my lips with a cloth napkin.

"If you say so." Shay shrugs, which is as good as a *yes*. I can see her struggling not to glance up at me as she wolfs down shrimp and friend tofu. On Wednesdays, she tries very hard to keep from giving any indication that she might actually love me.

I hadn't noticed until now that there's music playing. Haydn, I believe. "Is this Karina Gauvin singing?"

Shay looks up in amazement. She must be impressed by the astute observation, because it takes her a good four seconds to hide her smile. Rising from her chair, she stands, waiting, her arms crossed against her chest. I know better than to dawdle. Dropping my chopsticks on my plate, I clear the table quick as a bunny.

Beneath Shay's suit jacket, she wears a black corset with angry-looking Asian birds embroidered in gold floss. She tosses her jacket and trousers over the back of her chair, but they slip to the floor when she hops up to sit on the table.

"Bring me my boots, little slut."

I waste no time hustling to the closet as fast as my high-heeled feet will carry me. Seating myself in Shay's chair, I slip a knee-high boot onto her right foot. She presses its heel into my thigh, applying painful pressure against my carefully-shaven leg. When I put a leather boot on her left foot, she opens her legs to let me do them up both at once. The scintillating sound of their zippers rouses goosebumps all over my skin.

Shay does not wear panties on Wednesdays. I watch her pussy lips open like rose petals to soak the perfectly polished mahogany table. The sight of her juices gets me so aroused I could pass out. There's a tingling sensation between my legs. With my male parts all tucked out of sight, I pretend it's my cunt itching to be fucked.

"You have the loveliest pussy I've ever seen," I tell Shay.

"So eat me already." With a distant expression, she stares into oblivion. "Quit wasting my time."

"Certainly." I bow between her thighs. "Anything you desire."

Sliding toward me, Shay leans her elbows behind her on the table and sets her feet on my chair's arms. Her face is stone cold, but her pussy lips quiver. They run with clear nectar, betraying her remote demeanor. She can pretend all she likes, but I can plainly see how turned on she's getting as she waits for my lips to greet hers.

The aroma of her beautiful pussy is barely perceptible over the bouquet of my posh perfume, but that subtle combination of fragrances has me drooling for my wife's sweet cunt. I lean forward to kiss Shay's lower lips and she sucks air through her teeth.

I'll admit—unsexy as it sounds—it takes conscious effort not to worry about messing my make-up. When I flick Shay's clit with my tongue, I can taste my lipstick on her tender bud. That aroma of fruity wax sends me soaring to new heights of arousal. My lipstick on my wife's clit: Heaven! Hell, if my make-up wears off that's just one more excuse to put on more.

"Suck my clit," Shay commands, but I'm already halfway there. Diving between her legs, I wrap my hands around her calves garbed in smooth leather.

"Suck it, little whore."

I take her clit in my mouth and suck it like a cock. She keeps her lips shut tight, but I can tell by the little squeaking noises she's making that she's massively getting off. Shoving her wet pussy in my face, she tries to hold back exhilarated cries. Her futile attempt to suppress that crazy pleasure sounds a lot like a kettle on the boil. I could write a book: *My Wife, The Kettle.*

"What do you find so vastly amusing?" Shay roars.

"Nothing at all," I lie, flashing my lashes to prove my darling innocence.

"That's what I thought."

She's never satisfied by my responses.

I'm sure my make-up is a disaster, because she's half-smirking at my lips. Or perhaps it's the pussy juice coating my chin that's got her so pleased with herself.

Her demeanor hardens a touch. "I didn't say stop."

Diving back in, I devour Shay's pussy. She leans her elbows against the table and tosses her head back. Bucking her cunt against my hungry lips, she impedes an explosion of pleasure-cries as I ravage her clit. Finally, she can't take it anymore. Her body writhes and jumps against the sleek mahogany. She bites her lip until it bleeds.

*A woman knows what a woman wants.*

"Time for your humiliation, little slut." She lies, panting, on our dining room table. "Get me my cock."

If I had a pussy, it would be drooling.

In my lovely heels, I hop to the bedroom to retrieve my wonderful wife's strap-on harness and the big dildo she loves to fuck me with. I grab the lube as well, knowing we'll need it. As much as I would enjoy our Wednesday dinners even without getting screwed up the ass, it certainly adds an exciting dimension to the evening.

When I arrive back at her side, Shay is still reclined on the table. "Took you long enough."

"My humble apologies," I reply, offering the strap-on like a sacrificial blade. A thrill tingles up and down my spine as I make the presentation. "I brought your cock."

"A lot of good it'll do in your worthless hands, unless you plan on fucking yourself."

"Goodness no," I giggle, my voice escaping into the upper limits of its register. Setting the lube down on the table, I assure her, "That's a right reserved only to you."

Shay eyes the dildo and harness, tendering no response.

"If you'll do me the honour..." If I seem desperate, will she deny me pleasure out of spite?

"Suit me up," she instructs. "Come on, little bitch. Make me hard."

I do as I'm told, stumbling with excitement as I buckle her into the harness. Her dildo sticks straight up in the air as she lies on the table, and I can't wait for my wife to plough me with it.

Shay's teeth gleam, frightfully white. As her hand wanders the length my inner thigh, my heart palpitates. I can hardly breathe.

"Hike up your skirt," she instructs.

I hesitate. My panties serve the function of keeping my boy parts in check, but they aren't meant to be seen.

"Do it."

So I do. I collect the satin fabric of my long gown and hold it against my chest while Shay eyes my legs. Good thing I shaved.

"Now take those off," Shay demands. "Do it."

As I shift and shimmy out of my tight undergarment, my boy parts become untucked. They hang between my thighs like meat in a butcher shop window, and I feel my cheeks glowing crimson with embarrassment. I let my panties fall to the floor, feeling very vulnerable in my state of partial nudity.

"What is this?" Shay surprises me by grabbing my soft cock. "This useless mass of flesh here, what is this supposed to be?"

I try to speak, but the words stick like a fishbone at the back of my throat.

Without letting go, she slides to the edge of the table and sits up straight. "Answer me when I ask you a question."

With deep shame, I admit, "That's my cock."

The malice slips from Shay's bold expression. Of all the ways she could possibly react, she surprises me by laughing.

"This isn't a cock." She tugs it in her little fist. "Cocks get hard. See this here? See it?"

I fight not to respond as she wags her strap-on in my direction. "Yes, I see."

"This is what a *real* cock looks like," she says, stroking her monster dong. "I'd've thought a little slut like you could identify real meat by now."

"I apologize," I reply. That's all I have to offer.

"This!" She places the emphasis on my reprehensible little penis. "This is nothing. It's worse than nothing. A pussy, I could fuck. This is just useless. Get rid of it."

I don't want to look at my cock right now, but without my panties it's impossible to tuck it away. Now I'm taking too long fiddling with my balls. Shay's breathing down my neck, so to speak. She makes me nervous, and I fumble.

Running her fingers along my shoulder, she grabs me by the scruff of the neck. "Get rid of those things or I'll get rid of them for you."

Tucking my cock and balls up into my pelvis, I manage to get everything held in place so Shay won't have to look at my male parts. I can see why she hates them: they're ugly and crude. That's why I keep them hidden on Wednesday evenings. Shay deserves the best. She shouldn't have to look at my hideous body.

Shay must be able to see how flustered I've become, because her voice softens a touch as she commands me to *taste it*.

Grinning, I gaze at Shay's fingers as they grip the base of her dildo.

"You want to taste my big cock, don't you?"

"Yes," I cry, my mouth watering. "May I, please?"

"You'd better," Shay growls. "If your pretty little lips aren't planted around my cockhead in the next five seconds, you don't want to know what'll happen next."

It's an empty threat, of course, because I would never dream of resisting her.

Shay holds the dong steady as I lunge for it. This is what I sit at my desk fantasizing about all week: the moment the tip of my tongue meets her cold, hard cock. I don't taste anything at first, not until Shay lets go of the dildo to grab both my ears. She squeezes my clip-on earrings and the pressure on my tender lobes makes me shriek in pain. The sting convinces me I'm tasting precum, and her strap-on is an engorged slab of male meat.

"You like that, do you, little cocksucker?"

I nod my head as I work it with my tongue, but too soon she pushes my shoulders away. Her dong bounces as she slides from the table. The heels and toes of her big boots tap when she lands against the hardwood.

"Assume the position," she commands, her voice calm but firm. She slaps my bare ass as I bend over, holding my privates in place with one hand and hiking my dress up with the other.

Running her fingernails across my bum, she gives it a firm squeeze. Shay has a habit of setting her cockhead against my ass, and then splattering a load of lube in the small of my back. She pokes at my dry asshole, applying just enough pressure to keep us both tempted until the lube melts a pathway between my ass cheeks.

When the lube meets the bulbous head of her dildo, Shay wastes no time pressing it into me. She enters my asshole like a stampede, her shaft charging through my tight ass ring. I won't lie: it burns like hell for the first couple thrusts, but I know in a moment or two I'll begin to relax.

"You like getting fucked up the ass, don't you?" Shay breathes in my ear. "Don't you? You're just an anal-obsessed little whore, aren't you?"

"Oh yes," I hiss.

The initial sting subsides, and now my ass wants to devour her slick dildo. I can't keep my boy parts bundled up in my palm anymore; my cock grows bigger every time Shay ploughs me. I release it, gripping the table instead. Sure my cock is throbbing, just begging to be played with, but god only knows what my wife will do if she catches me fiddling with myself.

Shay grips my hips as she reams my asshole, and it feels so dirty and good that I push back against her to pump up the intensity. She's ploughing me so deep I want to scream. The urge to fondle my balls becomes impossible to resist, so I reach down and give them a squeeze. The pressure on those fuzzy spheres feels so incredible that I want to give myself more.

"You're just a little cum dumpster, aren't you?" As Shay leans in to whisper, her corseted tits brush my back and have to squeeze my tip to keep from coming. "You want me to fill your ass with jizz, don't you?"

"Yes!" I reply. "Yes, please pump me full of cum."

Growling, Shay plants her boots firmly to the floor. When she straightens to pump me from behind, I can't resist the call of my engorged cock. Wrapping layers of satin skirt around my hard shaft, I give it a soft stroke. My knees go weak. Thank goodness for the mahogany table keeping me upright.

"I'm too huge for you, am I?" Shay mocks, slowing her pace. "You can't take my massive rod?"

"I can take it," I assure her, afraid she'll pull out if I don't. "I love it when you fuck me hard. Please, it feels so good."

She pauses for a moment that feels like hours. "Very well, little tramp."

As she works her way back to full speed, I grip my cock firmly between the layers of my gown. When I pump it in time with Shay's thrusting, it feels like her dildo is reaming straight through me, and I'm yanking it off on the flip side. That's the only way I can do this: pretend this cock wrapped in satin isn't mine at all. It's Shay's, and I'm jerking on it for her pleasure.

Plunging into my ass, Shay launches every abusive epithet she can come up with. My thighs tremble and I know I won't last much longer. When I collapse on the table, my breast forms press into my chest. She tells me it's time to come.

Tugging fast as my hand will let me, I encourage my resistant body to release its tension. I visualize the cum shooting from Shay's loins, running clear through my ass and out my cock on the other side.

Pulling out of me, Shay breathes a sigh of exertion and collapses. Warm cream pools in the satin surrounding my spent cock, wetting the tip as it settles into the fabric. This gown is heading straight for the cleaners.

"What's so funny?" I ask, when I notice a smirk bleeding across my wife's lips.

"Oh, nothing." Shay sighs, toying with the everlasting monster between her legs. "I was just considering what it might be like if we went *out* for dinner one Wednesday night."

"I've thought about that too," I admit, circling my fingers around the base of her proud dildo. "But there isn't a restaurant in town that serves my favourite dessert."

# Shower Power

I'm not sure what woke me.

I'm thinking it was the birds outside our window. That's not something I experienced at home. Sometimes I could hear pigeons cooing on my neighbour's balcony, but never twittering sparrows or robins, or whatever was out in those trees.

Talia took up more space in bed than I did. She'd kicked the covers down to her feet. She was just a big naked body beside me, beckoning my hands.

My sleepy fingers moved across her thigh, and she moaned gently as I dipped between her legs.

Ooh, was her pussy wet!

"What have you been dreaming about?" I whispered, pressing my breasts against her arm.

"Hmm?"

She was naked, but I had on a little silk number. It was so thin it was like wearing nothing at all. I could feel the heat of Talia's skin right through it.

But nothing could compare with the heat of her pussy.

"You must have been dreaming something sexy," I told her. "You're all wet down here."

She cooed as I rubbed her clit in fat, lazy circles. "Oh honeybun, I gotta pee."

"Me too," I told her.

But she didn't get out of bed. She didn't even open her eyes as I wrapped my hand around her mound and squeezed.

She did smile, though.

And she said, "Cassie, I'm about to pee all over your hand."

"Go ahead," I said, challenging her. "You wouldn't dare."

Her eyelids fluttered. "Oh, wouldn't I?"

"Nope. Because you'd wet the bed, and you wouldn't want the maid to come in and be like... what a disgusting couple of lesbians!"

Talia chuckled sleepily, then pushed me away. "Okay, enough of that. Come take a shower with me."

I hopped out of bed giddily and took her hand when she reached for mine. She led me into the bathroom, but when I walked toward the toilet, she pulled me away from it.

"What do you think you're doing, little girl?"

"Going pee?" I asked.

She shook her head sternly. "Not in there you're not."

"Not in the toilet?"

She gave me that look—the one that made my legs quake. Then she reached into the shower and turned on the water. "You pee when I tell you to pee."

My belly felt like it was full of butterflies, in addition to a night's worth of water. Whenever she commanded me like that, I turned into a big puddle of lust. My body's functions were supposed to be, in some sense, automatic—or at least controlled by me. And here was my girlfriend, telling me I could only pee when she gave the word.

Maybe that doesn't sound like a turn-on, but it was.

Talia tore off my silk and pulled me into the shower, which was a bit of a shock. More the music of it than the sensation. The sound of water raining down and smacking the metal tub made me have to pee so much more than before.

"I have to go," I told my girlfriend. "I have to go really badly."

She pulled me closer, so the shower struck us both. It soaked my hair and refreshed my skin, which was sweaty from sleep. I raised my hands above my head and let the water wash my armpits. I splashed the clean, fresh cascade across my face while Talia unwrapped a bar of soap behind my back.

"How are you feeling now?" Talia asked.

"Good," I said. "But I still have to pee."

"Perfect." She traced the soap up my back and down my butt. Then she turned me around and said, "Ride my thigh, honeybun."

Straddling her leg, I asked, "Like this?"

"Push your pussy against my skin." She adjusted my body until my slick lips spread and my clit pushed down on her thigh. "That's it, little girl. Very good. Now move."

"Move?"

"Ride my thigh."

I hesitated. "But I have to pee. Really badly."

"Not my problem," she said, moving her thigh under my cunt. "Feel that? Feels good, doesn't it?"

"Yeah," I admitted.

She made her body soapy. "Touch me, Cassie. Make me come."

"Okay," I said, though that was a bit of an imposing expectation. "I'll try."

"Don't *try*. Do it."

Shoving her wet snatch at my hand, she grinded against my palm. She threw her head back and shook, splashing me, splashing the tile wall and the shower curtain.

Then she looked down and asked, "Why aren't you moving?"

"Moving?"

"Move!"

Oh, on her thigh. I'd forgotten the instruction.

I tried going at her hard enough to build toward an orgasm, but every time I slid my clit up and down her leg I had to pee even worse. I needed to stop. If I kept going I'd lose control of my bladder.

"Why'd you stop?" Talia asked.

I told her, "I'm gonna pee."

"Keep going."

"But I'll pee all over you!"

"Keep going!"

I couldn't argue with that logic.

To tell the truth, I didn't even want to argue. I just wanted to scrub my poor sweet pussy against my girlfriend's thigh until... oh God... I couldn't keep it in...

As I slid down Talia's thigh, pee escaped me.

I went all over her dark skin, splashing a new kind of wetness across the trail of juice I'd left there.

Pee streaked toward her hip, but it didn't get all the way there. It cascaded back again, tumbling down the side of her thigh and dripping to the base of the tub. There, it mixed with shower water and went from mellow yellow to crystal clear.

"It's warm," Talia said. "Warmer than the shower."

"I want to know what it feels like," I told her as I rubbed her pussy with my hand.

"Are you sure?" she asked.

"Yes."

"Be careful what you wish for."

"I am being careful."

She bowed to me as my stream dwindled to nothing. She touched her forehead to mine and said, "Good."

That's when I felt something warm and wet on my hand. On my fingers first, and then pooling in my palm.

Talia was peeing on me. She was peeing in my hand.

At first, I wasn't sure what to do. Just experience it? Do nothing and wait for it to be over, then decide after the fact whether it was something I'd want to do again?

No, I couldn't do nothing.

As she peed on my palm, I shoved two fingers inside her very wet snatch. She jumped, just a touch, but enough that her stream waved in the air and landed hot on my wrist.

She peed down my arm as I fucked her with my fingers. I had the worst craving to mash my palm against her clit, but I could just imagine pee splashing all over the place. I liked where it was falling on my arm.

I liked that a lot.

Talia grabbed my cunt and squeezed while I fingerfucked her. We went at each other hard, and I had a feeling she wished I was still peeing.

When her stream dwindled to drips, I must admit, I mourned the loss.

This was a first, for us. We'd just peed on each other. We'd never done that before. We'd never even talked about it.

But now that we'd done it once, I had a sneaking suspicion we'd do it again.

In the shower felt safe. Water cascaded down on us from above, washing away every trace of urine. Just to be sure, Talia and I washed each other thoroughly with soap. She made me come in no time, and when I worked on her hot body, she fell to her knees with an orgasm that seemed to worship the creator of all things sex.

Once we'd washed away the soap suds, Talia turned off the water. I fetched her a towel, then got one for myself.

"Thank you," she said, wiping her eyes first, then the rest of her face. "So, what did you think of that?"

I knew she was talking about the pee, and I said, "Unexpected. But very welcome."

# Mistress Audrey

I was just about to fold the laundry when someone rapped at the door. Who do you think was standing on the other side when I looked through the peephole?

That's right. It was Lawrence.

Why would he knock? He had a key! Worse than that, he was four hours early. I scrambled to straighten up the place, but it was no use. I'd planned on greeting him in fishnets and the leather bustier I'd just bought, but, *calisse*, no time for that now. And yes, I had far too much lingerie as it was, but the little black corset had been marked down to ten dollars. How could I resist?

"I wasn't expecting you until seven thirty," I said, after unlocking the security latches and swinging open the front door. Something was wrong. I could tell by the bleak look on his face. He seemed older, somehow. Defeat resounded in his voice as he informed me he couldn't stay.

"Excuse me?" I scathed. My tone was so frosty I could almost see little comic book icicles hanging off my words. It was Veronica's response when Archie breaks a date and she just knows he'll be going out with Betty instead.

"Ruth decided to stay home from the conference after all."

Those words landed like a kick in the gut. Teetering over rage on one side and despondence on the other, I tried not to shout or whine. "But we were supposed to spend the whole weekend together..."

Saying the words destabilized me, tossing me clear off the tightrope. I couldn't believe how enraged I was with Lawrence over something beyond his control. After all, it wasn't his fault his wife planned to be away that weekend, then decided to stay home at the last minute. And who was *I* to feel angry towards Ruth? Wasn't she the real victim in all this? But *merde*, this sort of thing happened every time we planned to be together. *Every fucking time!* I couldn't get over it.

"I know. I'm sorry," Lawrence mumbled, his gaze tracing the up-and-down, back-and-forth pattern of my parquet floors. He knew I was pissed. That's why he wouldn't look at me, like if he didn't look at me I wouldn't yell.

"*Tabernac!* We've been planning this for weeks, Lawrence. There are other things I could have been doing today, you know. I cancelled dinner with my brother and Susan to spend time with you."

"How is your brother?"

"Don't make small talk!" I fumed. I hated small talk. It was Lawrence's method of getting me off-track. "We finally arrange a weekend together and you have to go and fuck it up. Every time, Lawrence! Do you remember what happened last time? You promised we would finally get to spend a whole night in the same bed. Do you remember what you did?"

Lawrence wasn't looking at me. He was gazing at the basket of laundry in the middle of my living room. "I fell down the stairs," he responded.

"You fell and split your head open and had to go to the fucking emergency room to get stitches. You drive me nuts,

Lawrence. It's self-sabotage! We're never going to spend a whole night together, are we?"

"We will, just not this weekend," he assured me. Of course, I didn't believe him for a second. How could I?

My blood boiled over and became spite when it hit the air. *Why did I have to feel so angry?* So I couldn't have what I wanted right away. Why couldn't I just let it go? And then an unwelcome thought occurred to me. "Ruth didn't really stay home from her conference, did she? You met somebody else..."

He looked somewhat disgusted as he cried, "No!"

"...and you'd rather spend the weekend with her than with me."

"No! Audrey, listen to me," he replied, kicking off his shoes and shuffling me over to the couch strewn with laundry. "I would never do that to you. I love you. I'm here right now because I love you and I wanted to tell you in person that I can't stay."

*Can't stay?* Because he had to meet up with his new whore, perhaps? No, Lawrence would never do that to me. He wouldn't. Although, Ruth probably thought the same thing and I knew for a fact he was cheating on her. I knew because he was cheating with me. And, ultimately, whether he was leaving my apartment to see some new chick or to go home to his wife, it all boiled down to the same sediment. Somebody else was more important than me. Somebody else was *always* more important than me.

From the clean laundry I'd planned on folding, I plucked a burgundy knee-sock. "You're not going anywhere," I said flatly. Pulling Lawrence's Stratford Festival T-shirt over his head, I tied his wrists together in front of his body.

Lawrence laughed nervously as I unbuckled his belt, unzipped his fly and let his Dockers fall to the floor. "I don't really have time to make love today. I have to get home."

My teeth clenched. My heart turned to ice. Those words, *make love*, grated on my nerves. Did Lawrence ever make love to me, or was it all just good old fucking? He was supposed to spend the weekend with me, and now he didn't even have five minutes for a quickie?

"You think I want to *make love* with you, *putain de chien*?" I spat at my prisoner.

Confused as a kicked puppy, Lawrence retreated into himself. "Why would you call me that?"

"You don't even know what it means!"

"I know it's something bad."

"You are such a *maudit* liar! You lie to your w—" Never could say that word, the w-word. "...to *her* about me, now you're lying to me about this," I said, pulling his black Jockeys to his ankles. *The calm before the storm...*

"I'm not lying," he pleaded.

I believed him, but I needed some reason for my rage. How could I admit to being mad at Lawrence because he was married? I knew that from the moment we met, and I practically forced him into this arrangement. Well, yes, he wanted it too, but it took some convincing at first.

"Shut up!" I roared, forcing him down on the couch with his knees on the seat cushions and chest against the sofa back. Heading into my bedroom, I added, "A man who's already cheating on his wife has zero credibility in the trust department."

Stripping off my jogging pants and mint green sweater, I slipped into my thigh-high fishnets and black thong. I dressed up more for myself than for Lawrence, though I imagine he enjoyed it too.

"That's different," he implored from the next room. "There's nobody else. There's never been anyone but you."

"Aside from your wife," I replied acridly, chewing the plastic tag from my new leather garment. There was silence for a moment—a welcome change. Lawrence could be such a child at times.

"I love you, Audrey," he bleated like a pathetic little lamb.

*Whatever.*

As I zipped up the bustier, I suddenly realized why it had been marked down to ten dollars from two hundred and ninety-five. *Shit de merde*, I couldn't breathe! Why hadn't I tried it on before buying? I zipped it down halfway. Still a little constrictive, but better.

"You have no idea how disappointed I feel," Lawrence whined. "You have no idea how much I wanted to stay here with you tonight."

*I* had no idea? How many years had I looked forward to any opportunity to spend a night together? Yes, the raw animal sex was incredible, but without being able to spend an entire night basking in the afterglow, there was something missing. Lawrence and I weren't like other couples, and I was okay with that at first. *But now?* God, what I wouldn't give to have a normal life with him. This was supposed to be our one weekend of living like a regular couple, and he had to go and destroy it! Just like last time. How did Lawrence always manage to ruin everything?

"Shut up!" I nearly sobbed, grabbing assorted sex toys and paraphernalia from the night table and returning to the living room. Why could I never come up with anything really cruel to say when I was angry? It tried to come up with some insult...

"I'm sorry," he replied, eyes downcast as I strode by the sofa.

Lawrence drove me crazy with his incessant apologies. It was impossible to pick a fight with that man! Sometimes all I wanted was a good row, but he would never engage. My anger rolled off him like water from a duck's back.

"I can't stand you sometimes," I said in a voice so deep and cold I couldn't believe it was my own. "You're like a toilet: I shit all over you and you just take it."

The sides of Lawrence's lips turned upward. Okay, I probably could have phrased that better. It was, at best, a failed attempt at cruelty. The naked man on my couch was obviously trying to contain his mirth, but I was not in the mood to be chortled at. "Look at my face, Lawrence. Do I look like I'm laughing? Because I'm not."

His gaze rose from my parquet flooring, but didn't make it to my face. It lingered over my fishnet-clad legs, then my black lace thong, but what really caught his attention was the leather bustier. Sure, I couldn't breathe, but my boobs were bustin' out all over! I'd always wanted to be a dominatrix, and Lawrence was in dire need of punishment.

"I said, look at my *face*!" I growled, on principle. I actually liked that he was staring at my tits. They were on the small side, so it didn't happen all that often.

Guilty as a kid with his hand in the cookie jar, Lawrence gazed up and looked into my eyes. Had there been any hair on his beautiful bald head, I would have latched onto it and pulled. Instead, I walked around the sofa and soaked in the view. Lawrence still had a great ass left over from his marathon-running days. It was peachy, muscular, and tight, but with just enough give that, when my palm made contact with it, the flesh rippled for a moment.

Lawrence turned his head around as best he could, tied up as he was. "You hit me," he whimpered, shocked at my violence.

"I *spanked* you. There's a difference," I said flatly. Inside I was bouncing off the walls, but my face was stone. I wouldn't crack. When my palm fell once again against Lawrence's ass, I kept an eye on his undecided cock. It jerked forward.

"Looks to me like you're enjoying this," I accused, warming his cheeks in circles with my hands. Standing directly behind Lawrence, I smacked both cheeks at once and his whole body jerked forward.

"Maybe. I don't know," he murmured. How was that for an uncommitted response? My hands travelled down his smooth ass-cheeks and through the tunnel of his spread thighs to find his cock rigid and ready. I squeezed it. Hard. The muscles in his thighs stiffened.

"You're going to get your filthy pre-come all over my couch, *putain de chien*." I said with a cruel grin. From the laundry basket on my floor, I plucked a bath towel and spread it out beneath his cumbersome form.

"You don't need to call me names," Lawrence objected.

Blessed are the meek...

"Don't I, liar?" I asked, smacking his ass harder than before.

"*Ow*. I've never lied to you!"

"But you lie to your w..." I trailed off. *Silence.*

That's when the clothes pegs next to my laundry hamper spoke to me. Pinching his flesh first between my fingers, I clamped a springy wooden peg onto each of his thighs.

"*Ow!*" Lawrence shrieked. "What are you doing to me?" His initial impulse was to rub the pegs together, but that only made them pull tighter on his skin. *Silly rabbit.*

"Clothes pegs, cheater!" I scowled.

"Oh," he reacted, as though I'd come up with the idea all on my own and not seen it online. He didn't tell me to take them off, so I clamped on two more pegs and watched the villain's asshole twitch. *I'll get to you, my pretty...*

I'd never bitten Lawrence before. His flesh was too taut to really chomp down on, but I got my point across by sinking my teeth into his ass. He pulled away, but didn't get far. Then, without thinking, I kissed the hurt I'd created. I obviously wasn't getting the hang of the whole dominatrix thing.

"*Ow!* Audrey, honey, I've never cheated on you..."

I spanked him again. Hard.

"And I never would."

*Smack.*

*Why should I believe that?* My muscles trembled until I let loose on Lawrence's sweet ass. Five, six, seven times? I lost count. When I saw how red his bottom was, I stopped. Maybe I was hurting him more than I intended, and more than I ought.

Reaching up to his head, I petted just above his neck as something of a peace offering. Lawrence was like a puppy—he liked to be scratched behind the ears. Digging into his skin a touch, I dragged my nails down his back, leaving thin red lines all the way down to his tender ass. I leaned low, writhing against him so the smooth leather of my black bustier could salve his burning flesh.

Reaching under, I grabbed Lawrence's squishy balls and he inhaled sharply. He thought I was playing nice, that all was forgiven. *Not bloody likely.* I sank my teeth into his ass with full force, leaving two red semi-circles in my wake. Lawrence shrieked and jerked forward. But, hey, he had it coming.

"What are you doing to me?" he cried.

"Giving you what you deserve," I said, tugging the belt from his Dockers. He didn't say to stop. Folding the brown leather in two, I pulled the belt taut and it released a resounding crack. I could have whipped him right away, but I knew it would be more fun to generate suspense. Besides, all the domination had my pussy crying out for attention.

Making my way behind the sofa in the middle of my living room, I raised a leg up and over Lawrence's shoulder, holding the wretched villain in place. His mouth was perfectly aligned with my cunt, and I laced my makeshift whip around the back of his head. "Eat me, *cochon.*"

Lawrence licked my sensitive pussy lips through the lace of my thong. The wetness of his mouth mingled with my juices, making the area into a sopping mess. I could tell my clit was engorged, because I could feel Lawrence's warm tongue against it even through my underwear. I couldn't bear the resistance anymore. I instructed Lawrence to shift my thong out of the way.

"But my hands are tied," he whined.

"So use your nose, *emmerdeur!*"

I laughed inwardly as my partner of four years nudged my thong out of the way. He licked my pussy lips like a frightened animal.

"Not good enough!" I scolded, unfolding the leather belt. Raising it into the air, I held it up before finally working up the nerve to strike. When I cast it down against Lawrence's back, the *maudit* whip didn't even make contact. It just flipped to the side. I tried again. Same thing. *Really annoying!* I was trying to maintain a certain mystique and that belt was not co-operating.

But third time's a charm, and when I whipped him once again, the leather landed soundly against his back. He flinched, exhaling warm air against my hot cunt. It must have hurt him, but not very much. Not *enough*, I should say.

Next time, I didn't lift the belt so high into the air. I flipped it up and back down in one quick motion. The whip cracked with a heart-palpitating swish against my slave's back. That got him moving. The little licks he'd issued against my pussy lips turned into hard, lingering laps of my juice.

"How does that taste?" I asked.

"Mmm..." he mumbled.

I struck Lawrence's back with the whip. *That'll learn him.*

"Delicious," he corrected himself.

"That's right. Now kiss my cunt."

Lawrence gave my clit a peck. *That's not what I meant.* I whipped him again. His back was getting red now.

"Kiss it with your tongue, *putain de chien*!"

I whipped him once more and that did the trick. He infiltrated my achingly eager cunt with his tongue and I thought my knees were going to give out. His kisses were hot, his tongue solid and hard, flailing against the periphery of my pussy. Just to hear that *wha-chuk* sound again, I belted Lawrence's bare back. He stopped kissing and looked up at me, his chin gleaming with sticky nectar. He awaited instruction.

"Suck my clit," I said. "Suck it hard."

*God, did he ever!* I dropped the belt to hold his head in my hands. I didn't want to lose the scary dominatrix demeanour, but

I couldn't help myself. I whimpered as Lawrence vacuumed my clit into his mouth.

My hips began to move, to gyrate. I couldn't help it. It was like he was sucking my body out through my clit. It was wonderful. I could hardly breathe. *Oh, my bustier was too tight.* If I didn't take it off, I was going to collapse! As the leather top fell to the floor, I forced my cunt against Lawrence's face, writhing against his mouth. Grabbing hold of his shoulder, I dug my nails deep into his flesh. Couldn't help it.

"*Tabernac*, Lawrence!" I cried, teetering on the brink of insanity. "You are fucking incredible!"

I fell away from his glistening mouth, my head spinning from too much pleasure, and Lawrence propped himself up to lick my cold breasts. The wetness and warmth of his tongue against my erect nipples made my body quiver. My knees were weak, but there was one more thing I wished to do to my prisoner before letting him escape.

Unclipping the clothes pegs from his thighs, I watched Lawrence's reddened flesh bounce back into place. From the basket of paraphernalia from my night table, I plucked some lube and an oddly-shaped contraption I'd bought online...*This popular item has the perfect contours to stimulate a man's prostate.* It was smooth with bulbous little offshoots, and the end had curved handles to make it easy to grip while you're ramming your partner with it. We'd never used this thing before. Lawrence didn't even know I had it.

"How hard are you?" I asked my slave, standing behind him.

"I would say *very*," he responded.

"Well, you have two choices. I can whip you or I can fuck you."

"Oh, fuck me, please!" he said like a kid in a candy store.

I laughed. "No, I don't think you understand."

When I held the strange dildo in front of his face, Lawrence looked dubiously back at me. "What is that?"

"Do you want to find out?"

His smile was hesitant. "I think I'd rather be whipped."

I smiled with saccharine insincerity. "Suit yourself." Picking up his belt up off the couch, I laid it down across his back. *Wha-chuk! Wha-chuk! Wha-chuk!* I struck him as hard as I could manage, every blow falling on the same tender strip of skin.

"Stop!" Lawrence cried. "Okay, okay. Try the other thing."

Well, that was one way to settle a dispute. Slathering the toy in lube, I massaged the excess into his twitching asshole. Lawrence released a low moan. "Are you going to... you know...?"

Jerk him off?

"I want to hear you beg for it," I replied.

"Please!"

"Please what? I can't read your mind," I teased. Of course I could.

"Audrey, could you *please* stroke my cock?"

"Well, since you asked so nicely..."

That settled it: I was an absolute failure as a dominatrix. *Oh well.* Reaching around his lovely ass, I took firm hold of his rigid rod and Lawrence was putty in my hands. He moaned and whispered my name, thrusting his hips so his cock ran smoothly through my fist. I set the end of my new toy against his convulsive asshole and jiggled it about. He sighed at the slight pressure I exerted.

He wouldn't last long. There was no time to lose. I pressed hard on the slippery toy, but his ass was too resistant. The harder I pushed, the more Lawrence tightened up and whimpered. He stopped thrusting his hips.

"Relax," I encouraged my little anal virgin, smoothing my fingers over his cock-head, pumping hard against it.

I tried again with the toy, but it wasn't happening.

"I'm sorry, Audrey. I'm trying, but it feels like a blunt instrument."

Had I been a good dominatrix, I would have forced the prostate pleaser into his ass, hard, and ignored his cries. I just couldn't do that to Lawrence. As much pain as he caused me, I could never hurt the man. I set the toy aside.

With a good dollop of lube on my finger, I found his curious asshole and tickled it. When I issued only the slightest pressure, Lawrence's elastic hole opened up like Ali Baba's cave.

"Oh, wow!" Lawrence gushed as I stroked his warm insides. "That's incredible."

"That's my finger."

"Maybe that's why," he replied. "It's person-to-person."

I wasn't sure what he meant, but I kept on petted his prostate. Lawrence whimpered and whined like an animal. That's how I knew he was really getting off—he was usually so quiet. His modest cock jerked and twitched under my throttlehold. When his thighs began to tremble and quake, I knew he wasn't long for the world of the inorgasmic.

*Oh, ah, oh! Audrey! Oh, Audrey! Oh, Audrey!*

It was like seeing my name in lights. Lawrence's voice honoured each consonant, each vowel, and always *y*. His body tightened up and his ass clamped down against my finger. He might have sucked it into his body if it hadn't been attached to my hand. I could have sworn I felt the come burst up his shaft before it erupted from his tip in gushing spurts.

Covering his cock-head with my palm, I massaged the hot jizz against his straining rod.

"That was the most incredible..." Lawrence began. I waited to see if he was going to finish the thought, but no. Lawrence just collapsed on the couch, whimpered even more pathetically than when I'd whipped him. I untied his hands, but he remained draped over the sofa back.

Sitting down beside my Lawrence, I smoothed my hand over his rosy cheeks, along his side and his back. The first few soft touches generated tremors and spasms, but the more I petted his skin, the calmer he became. A despairing feeling weighed on my heart. This was the part I hated. "You have to go, don't you?" I asked him.

Turning his head, he cast a heavy gaze upon me. Lawrence's eyes were sky blue when he was happy, overcast when he was sad. At that moment, they were cloudy with a chance of rain. He nodded.

"But you wish you could stay?" I asked, eager for a compliment.

"I don't know," Lawrence replied, scrunching his nose. "If you spank me and whip me and stick things up my butt while I'm awake, what would you do to me in my sleep?"

Though I wanted to, I couldn't bring myself to laugh. "And you're going home, right? You're not going to spend the weekend with some other girl?"

"Audrey," Lawrence said, wrapping me in the warmth of his arms, "there's no one else but you."

I cackled wryly. "Give me a break, Lawrence. You have a wife! How could I...?"

"Audrey," he interrupted me. "There's no one else but you."

Perhaps stupidly, I believed him.

# Nailed

Mandy never used to hold my hand in the car. This was new, this one hand on the wheel, one pressed into my palm thing. I loved the innocent romance of it. Handholding was Betty and Veronica, complete with the love triangle. Ours was an all-female version, equally contentious, and focused entirely around big, beautiful Mandy.

Pink polish. Her fingernails were glossy, but they shimmered purple in the blue light from the dashboard. Every time we hit a bump in the road, they dug into the meat of my hand. It hurt so good.

But if I thought my kitten had claws in the car, that was nothing compared to the bedroom. Her daggers really came out when we got to my place. I brought out my thickest strap-on dildo and she dug those treacherous nails into my ass so hard I screamed.

She knew just how I liked my pain.

"God, that hurts." I wrapped my legs around hers and held her in my arms. "Feels incredible. But it hurts."

"Thought so."

"I love it, Mandy." I growled like a bear, bucked like a bull, until my dildo couldn't take the heat and popped right out of her pussy.

I slowed my thrusts, guiding that slippery shaft back inside her unfathomable wetness. After that, I fucked Mandy gently enough to stay inside. Cocks had minds of their own. Even fake ones.

She writhed beneath me, pushing her big tits against mine so our nipples played and pressed together. When kissed, she dug her nails into my flesh and squeezed. My body leapt and I gasped like pain was my oxygen.

"Too much?" she asked, teasing, knowing very well it wasn't.

"No, baby, feels good." I hugged her body tight, forcing my fake cock up inside her. The strap stroked my clit with every thrust, but there was a part of me that wished I could feel her pussy muscles clamping down on my dildo. If only there were artificial nerve endings I could hook up to feel that pressure.

Mandy's fingernails closed the sensation gap, and she must have known it.

"More," I pleaded. "Make it sore."

I wanted to feel the hurt all week. I wanted to feel it on the days she spent with Aisha instead of me. When I was alone in bed, wondering if Mandy was alone too—but too afraid to call and find out—I wanted to feel the sting of my girl's fingernails, a reminder that she loved me too. The pain would serve as a memento of our lust.

But Mandy teased me, tracing her nails up my back so lightly it tickled, making me shiver as I shoved my cock in her.

"Harder," I begged.

"I don't want to hurt you," she said, always teasing, taunting, dancing her fingernails across my skin.

"I *want* you to hurt me." I thrust in her, making her whimper and cringe and tighten the muscles in her thighs.

She hesitated, tracing her fingers down my ass, gently, too gently.

"It's not like anyone's going to see the marks," I said—a loaded statement, and she knew it. I could tell by the look in her eyes.

*Exclusivity.*

I'd tried not to push too hard, but she knew I wanted exactly what I offered. I wanted her to be mine and mine alone, just like I was hers. *Exclusively.* There was no other girl I wanted. Just Mandy. Why couldn't she be satisfied with just me?

The smile on Mandy's face did it. I bubbled from the inside out, kissing her cheeks, her nose, her lips as I rocked inside her. She dug her nails into my ass and I arched away from her mouth. Gasping, I cobra-posed on top of her full body and cried out, "Oh God!"

It hurt like hell, but I loved it. She was right about me. She was totally right.

"Sometimes I look at you," I said, "and my insides just feel like they're gonna come bubbling out."

She rolled her eyes like she didn't believe me, so I fucked her harder, sliding one hand around her front. Slipping it between our sweat-soaked bodies, I found her clit. Her eyelids fluttered closed as she arched. The sight of her like that, so close to ecstasy, made me want to stop everything and take a picture.

Then Mandy scratched ten red lines into my ass, and the sheer sting of it moved my hips in double time.

"I look at you, Mandy..." I grunted as I fucked her. "I look at you and my temperature rises. And then you touch me and I'm so hot I can't stand it."

She squinted, squealed, threw herself at my strap-on. "When you get hot, I get hot."

"Yeah?" I asked, grinding against the harness, getting myself off on the strap while she writhed beneath me.

"Oh yeah, baby."

Mandy dug those lacquered nails into my fleshy ass. My body heaved itself against hers. My hips went crazy. I knew I could get myself off like this. I was just about there. We could come together. We could do it.

"How hot are you now?" she asked, panting, her voice thin as linen.

"So fucking hot!" I growled.

Her razor nails dipped down the small of my back, slicing a path to my shoulders. The pain egged me on like a brand. I fucked her so hard she screamed, finding my ass once again and driving her nails into my flesh.

"You really like this, don't you?" She was laughing and panting at once.

There were no words to express how much I loved her nails. I loved the sharp stabs and lingering sizzle, so I kissed her, melting and melding into her mouth.

She tore me to shreds as we came together. The flood and gush of our orgasm took everything from me. All the energy I'd had was suddenly gone, and my thighs ached. We were drenched in sweat, panting, straining, drained.

I pulled out, letting my cock rest on her thigh as I lay on my side. Staring. God, she was beautiful with her hair stuck to her temples. She was so beautiful I could die.

My back shrieked with pain and I could just imagine how it would feel when I took a shower—the soap, the sting, the hot needling water. For some reason, that made me think about Aisha, and my mood dropped down into hell.

Mandy must have read my face, because she sighed. I thought I knew what she'd say: "Don't start," or maybe, "Just be happy we're together right now."

But I was wrong.

She said, "You know I love you."

"I know. I love you too." I kissed her chest, her shoulders, eager to show her just how much. I sucked her breasts, and for a moment she was quiet.

Then she said, "Aisha. I love her too."

I pulled away from Mandy's nipple and nodded. My bottom lip quivered, and I bit it until my mouth filled with the metallic sting of blood.

"But she's so jealous now," Mandy went on. "She never used to be. In the beginning, she was mature about our situation—like you are."

Usually, I didn't like hearing about Aisha, but hope swelled my heart. Did Mandy mean... was it over between them?

"I had to walk away," she said, and I felt the weight of her heartbreak in my chest. "Jealousy is relationship poison, and once it's in your veins that's the beginning of the end."

For the first time, I really understood how much Mandy loved both Aisha and me. I'd secretly painted our open relationship with a much blacker brush than it deserved. All this time, Mandy was full of love for us, but Aisha and I were too competitive to see each other's worth.

My back and my butt stung from Mandy's nails, but I couldn't enjoy the sensation just yet. Now that I had exactly what I *thought* I wanted, I realized I wanted more.

"You've got so much love to give," I told Mandy. "And you know what? So do I."

She looked at me and smiled like she knew just what I was going to say next.

"Let's talk to Aisha." I'd usually feel embarrassed to suggest it, but the marks Mandy left on my skin had opened me up to new possibilities. "Let's do more than talk."

"That's what you want?" Mandy asked, leaning up on her elbows.

I nodded. "If she wants it, I want it too. We could be good together, all three of us."

Mandy leaned in to kiss me softly, and then she whispered, "Aisha's got nails like the devil. You're going to love her, babe."

# You might also enjoy:

**Giselle's Best Fetish Erotica**
**14 Kinky Sex Stories**
By Giselle Renarde

FROM KINKY COSTUMES to sex dolls, Giselle's got you covered!

In this spanking-new collection, find fourteen tales of discipline and bondage, dressing up and role play, voyeurism, public sex, food and toys and so much more! Award-winning author Giselle Renarde has written erotic fiction for hundreds of anthologies, and her work is anything but ordinary. Giselle's Best Fetish Erotica includes quirky original stories and fantastic fan favourites to tickle unexplored regions of your sexual mind.

Surrender to temptation today!

*Find Giselle's Best Fetish Erotica at your favourite ebook retailer!*
*Also available in print!*

# ABOUT THE AUTHOR

Giselle Renarde is an award-winning queer Canadian writer. Nominated Toronto's Best Author in NOW Magazine's 2015 Readers' Choice Awards, her fiction has appeared in well over 100 short story anthologies, including prestigious collections like Best Lesbian Romance, Best Women's Erotica, and the Lambda Award-winning collection Take Me There, edited by Tristan Taormino. Giselle's juicy novels include Anonymous, Cherry, Seven Kisses, and The Other Side of Ruth.

**Giselle Renarde**
*Canada just got hotter!*
Want to stay up to date? Visit
http://donutsdesires.blogspot.com[1]!
Sign up for Giselle's newsletter: http://eepurl.com/R4b11
Weekly Audio Erotica at http://Patreon.com/AudioErotica

---

1. http://donutsdesires.blogspot.com/

2

---

2. http://patreon.com/AudioErotica

# Don't miss out!

Visit the website below and you can sign up to receive emails whenever Giselle Renarde publishes a new book. There's no charge and no obligation.

https://books2read.com/r/B-A-EGX-XEACF

**BOOKS 2 READ**

www.ingramcontent.com/pod-product-compliance
Ingram Content Group UK Ltd.
Pitfield, Milton Keynes, MK11 3LW, UK
UKHW021645190726
13853UKWH00001B/73